JEANNE TITHERINGTON

Sophy
and
Auntie Pearl

GREENWILLOW BOOKS, NEW YORK

One morning when Sophy woke up, she discovered she could fly.

"I can't wait to tell," she said to herself on the way to breakfast.

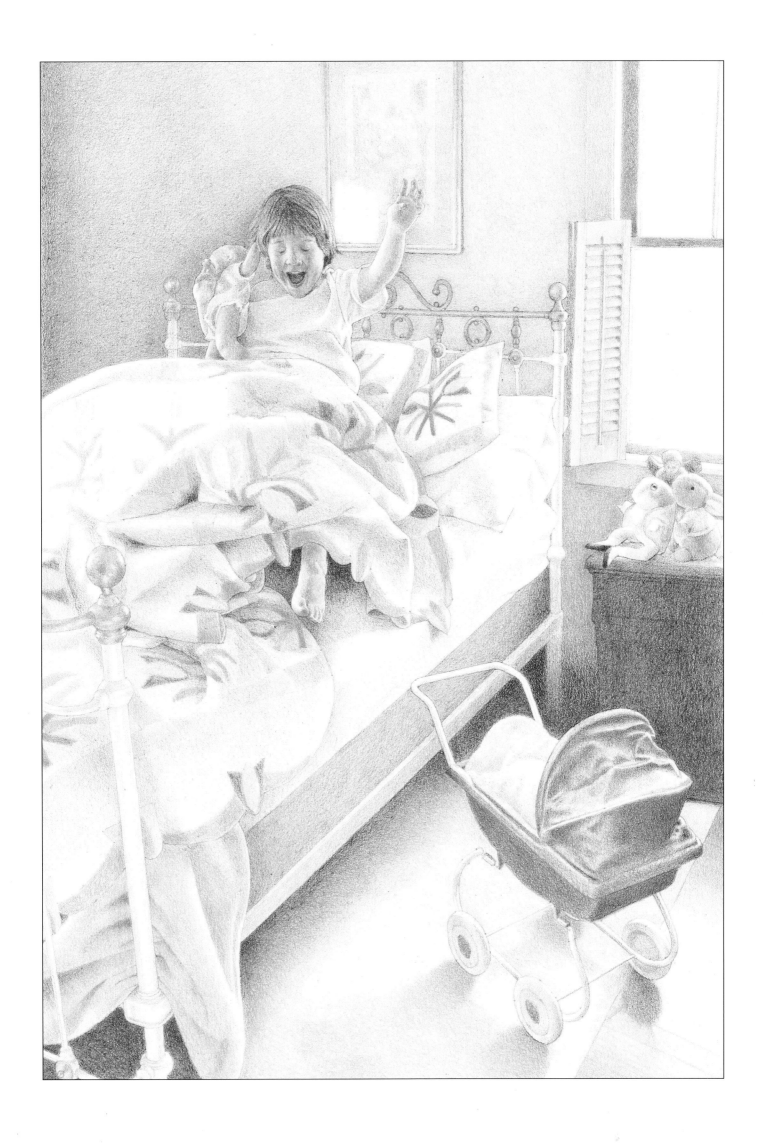

But Sophy's mother wasn't interested. "Drink your juice, Sophy," was all she said.

Sophy's father wasn't interested, either.

"That's nice, Sophy," he mumbled.

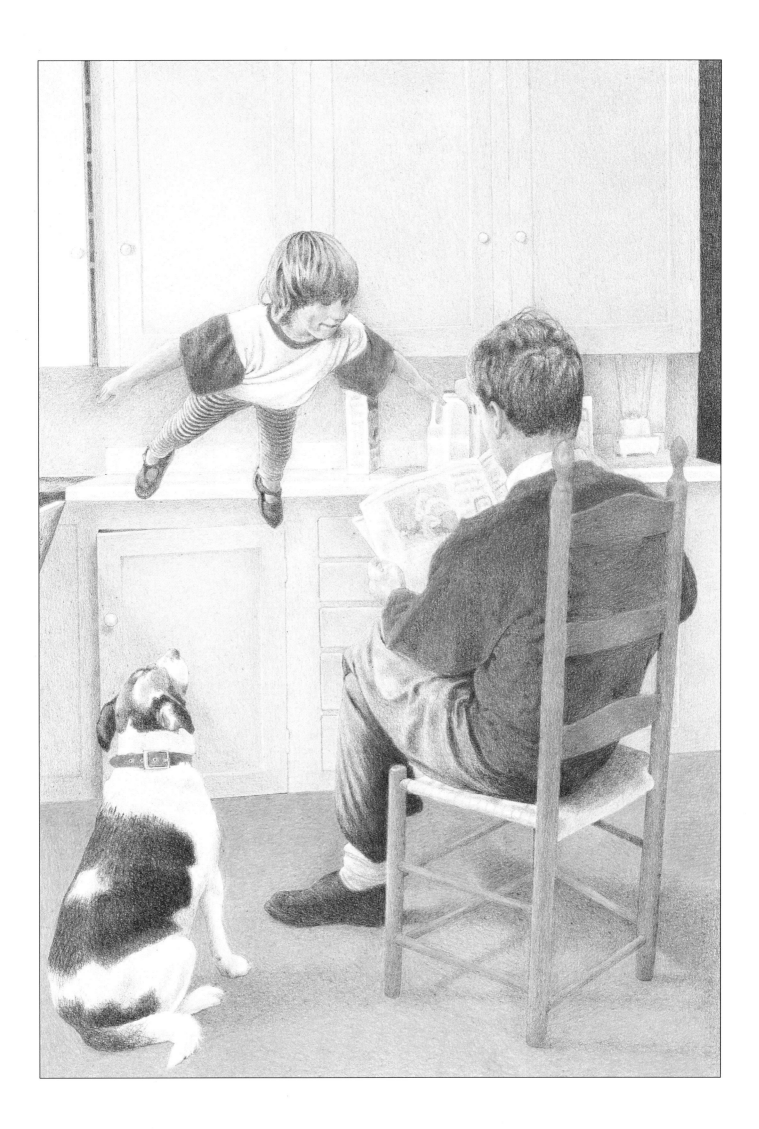

So Sophy rushed next door to tell Great-Aunt Pearl. "I can fly, Auntie!" she announced.

"Well, imagine that!" her great-aunt exclaimed. "I always knew you took after me."

"What do you mean, Auntie?" asked Sophy. "Can you fly, too?"

"Why, of course I can. We must go for an outing," said Great-Aunt Pearl.

So Auntie Pearl put on her favorite hat, and she and Sophy headed downtown.

It was such a pleasant day, they decided to take a roundabout route.

They passed through
the zoo. Sophy liked the
monkeys best, but Auntie
Pearl preferred the giraffes.

They ventured down
Main Street. Auntie Pearl,
being very fond of hats,
insisted on a bit of window
shopping.

They stopped outside
Timeless Toppers, which
was on the second floor
over the bookstore.

Quite exhausted, they stopped for ice cream. Sophy had a bubble gum cone, and Auntie Pearl had a large chocolate sundae.

On the way home Sophie said, "Auntie, do Mommy and Daddy know you can fly?"

"I told them once," her great-aunt answered, "but they didn't pay any attention."

"That's funny," said Sophy. "They didn't pay any attention when I told them, either."

"Just as well," her auntie replied.

And when they got home, no one noticed they'd been gone.

FOR JOHN GABRIEL,
WHOSE GRAMMY WATCHES OVER HIM

Colored pencils were used for the full-color art.
The text type is Carolina.
Copyright © 1995 by Jeanne Titherington
All rights reserved. No part of this book may be reproduced or
utilized in any form or by any means, electronic or mechanical, including
photocopying, recording, or by any information storage
and retrieval system, without permission in writing from the Publisher,
Greenwillow Books, a division of William Morrow & Company, Inc.,
1350 Avenue of the Americas, New York, NY 10019.
Printed in Singapore by Tien Wah Press
First Edition 10 9 8 7 6 5 4 3 2 1

Library of Congress Cataloging-in-Publication Data

Sophy and Auntie Pearl / by Jeanne Titherington.
p.   cm.
Summary: When she cannot get her parents to pay any attention,
Sophy shares her new-found ability to fly with her great-aunt.
ISBN 0-688-07835-4 (trade).   ISBN 0-688-07836-2 (lib. bdg.)
[1. Great-aunts—Fiction.   2. Flight—Fiction.]   I. Title.
PZ7.T53So   1995   [E]—dc20
94-22620   CIP   AC